My Father's Luncheonette

by Melanie Hope Greenberg

DUTTON CHILDREN'S BOOKS
NEW YORK

Dedicated to my parents, Larry and Ruth,
and my sisters, Barbara and Joni.

Special thanks to Jane, Lucia, On the Job, Judy,
Andy, The Promenade Diner, Larry's Luncheonette,
and rock 'n' roll.

Copyright © 1991 by Melanie Hope Greenberg
All rights reserved.
Library of Congress Cataloging-in-Publication Data

Greenberg, Melanie Hope.
    My father's luncheonette/by Melanie Hope Greenberg.—1st ed.
        p.   cm.
    Summary: A young girl enjoys a day of eating a fat, juicy burger,
dancing to the music of the jukebox, and mopping the floor at her
father's luncheonette.
    ISBN 0-525-44725-3
    (1. Restaurants, lunchrooms, etc.—Fiction.   2. Fathers and
daughters—Fiction.   3. Bronx (New York, N.Y.)—Fiction.)
I. Title.
PZ7.G82755My   1991   90-45586   CIP   AC
(E)—dc20

Published in the United States by
Dutton Children's Books,
a division of Penguin Books USA Inc.

Designer: Sylvie Le Floc'h
Printed in Hong Kong by South China Printing Co.
First Edition   10 9 8 7 6 5 4 3 2 1

My father's luncheonette is
twelve hops on my left foot,
eight hops on my right foot,
twenty-three skips,
and around the corner from where I live.

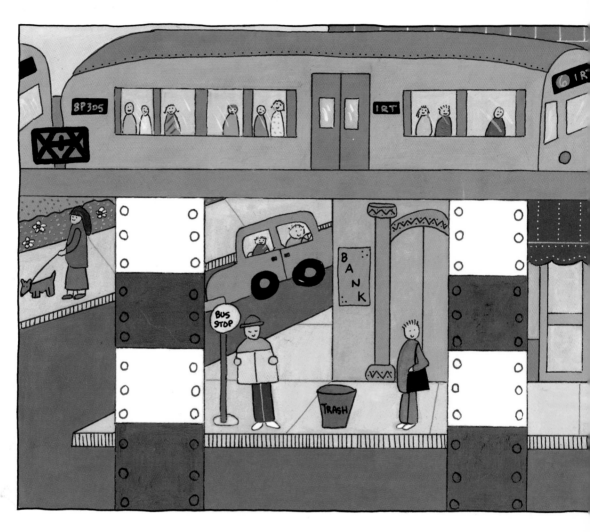

The noisy Number 6 train
rattles overhead as I race
past the South Bronx Savings Bank,

Abie's Hardware Store,
and Sandbanks Jewelry Shop.
Then I'm there.

People come to my father's luncheonette

for breakfast, lunch, and dinner.

When it is time for the lunch crunch,
my father flips a zillion burgers,
cooks up a million grilled-cheese sandwiches,
and fizzes up a thousand sodas.

But I am his best customer.
I love to order from the menu.
``I'll have a fat, juicy burger,
a bubbly egg cream, and your
very special squiggly French fries, please.''

I twirl around on the tall stool like a ballerina
while I wait for my dessert—
vanilla ice cream with chocolate sprinkles. Yum!

My best friend, Ronnie, loves to meet me
at the luncheonette. Today she can
order anything she wants. My treat!

We sit in the booth at the back.
Ronnie orders a Best Friend Special—
a square-scooped strawberry ice-cream soda
with rainbow sprinkles. My father makes it
just for her.

Then we dance to the jukebox—
Shing-a-Ling, Boog-a-Loo,
Mashed Potatoes, and the Twist.
My father always has dimes and
quarters to play the latest hits.

After Ronnie goes home, I clip
the Dinner Special signs to the menus.
Tonight's special is pot roast.

When Wanda the waitress takes her break,
I get to be the waitress. I bring
Wanda a glass of water and take her order.
I hope she orders toast.
It's the only thing I know how to make—

except my Super Special Playtime Potion.
I mix ketchup, sugar, raspberry syrup, mustard,
and ten spoonfuls of dishwater in a glass.
``A budding chef,'' my father says proudly.
He doesn't mind the mess.

After the last customer leaves,

we get ready to close my father's luncheonette.

It's mop-up time!

Steamy hot bubbles slush over black-and-white tiles.

When they are dry,
I hop, hop, hop on one foot
and never land on a white tile.

My father can finally sit down and relax.
I ask him,
``Can you help me with my homework now?''
And he always does.

On tiptoe, I can reach the switch
to turn off the neon light in the window.

Together we pull the door tight.
Then I twirl the key in the lock.

My father's luncheonette
is closed for the night.

Good night.